Magnificent Tales

Good News of Great Joy

The Amazing Story of Jesus' Birth

Based on Luke 1:26–2:14

Kelly Pulley

David C Cook

transforming lives together

GOOD NEWS OF GREAT JOY
Published by David C Cook
4050 Lee Vance View
Colorado Springs, CO 80918 U.S.A.

David C Cook Distribution Canada
55 Woodslee Avenue, Paris, Ontario, Canada N3L 3E5

David C Cook U.K., Kingsway Communications
Eastbourne, East Sussex BN23 6NT, England

The graphic circle C logo is a registered trademark of David C Cook.

LCCN 2012940693
ISBN 978-0-7814-0622-2
eISBN 978-0-7814-0850-9

Art and Text © 2012 Kelly Pulley

The Team: Susan Tjaden, Amy Konyndyk, Jack Campbell, Karen Athen

Manufactured in Hong Kong, in July 2012 by Printplus Limited.
First Edition 2012

1 2 3 4 5 6 7 8 9 10

071712

For Mary Pulley (Mom)

A young woman named Mary
got quite a surprise,
when an angel appeared
right in front of her eyes!

She was terribly frightened
as you would be too!
If what happened to her
had just happened to you!

The angel said,
"Mary, there's no need to fear.
You are special to God,
which is why I am here.
I bring you the message
that you are the one
who was chosen by God
to give birth to His Son."

Mary said, "I'm not married,
so how could this be?"
Then the angel told Mary,
"Trust God and you'll see."
So she trusted in God.
She said, "Lord, let it be."

Now Mary and Joseph
were soon to be wed.
Joseph dreamed of an angel
while sleeping in bed.

He was terribly frightened
as you would be too!
If what happened to him
had just happened to you!

The angel said,
"Joseph, there's no need to fear.
I've a message from God,
which is why I am here."

"The baby that Mary
now carries within
is Jesus,
God's Son,
who will pay for man's sin."

God's message was clear.
Joseph knew what to do.
So he married young Mary.
She married him too.

Soon they both had to travel to Joseph's hometown,
so the king's people-counters
could write their names down.
To Bethlehem Joseph and Mary were sent,
so they packed up some things
on their donkey and went.

But the town was so crowded,
there wasn't a room.
And the baby in Mary
was coming out soon!

Then the innkeeper said,
"There's a place you can rest.
As for beauty and comfort,
it's far from the best.

It's a stable where horses
and cows and sheep stay.
But at least there's a roof
and some dry, comfy hay."

That night Jesus was born
in the animals' stable,
where Joseph and Mary
did what they were able
to make Him a cozy,
warm, comfortable bed,
in a manger with hay
they fluffed up for His head.

Then they wrapped Him up tight in some soft
swaddling clothes, which made Him feel snug
from His head to His toes.

And the animals' lullabies
lulled Him to sleep,
with soft mooing of cows
and the bleating of sheep.

Nearby, shepherds were watching
their sheep in the night.
When an angel appeared!
All around them shone bright!

They were terribly frightened
as you would be too!
If what happened to them
had just happened to you!

The angel said,
"Shepherds, there's no need to fear.
I have brought you good news
of great joy you should hear!"

"Today in a manger
was born Christ the King!"
Then a great many more angels started to sing!
They appeared all around,
singing praises and then,
they sang, "Glory to God,
Peace on earth to all men!"